The King and the Gifts of Gold

Georg Dreissig and Maren Briswalter

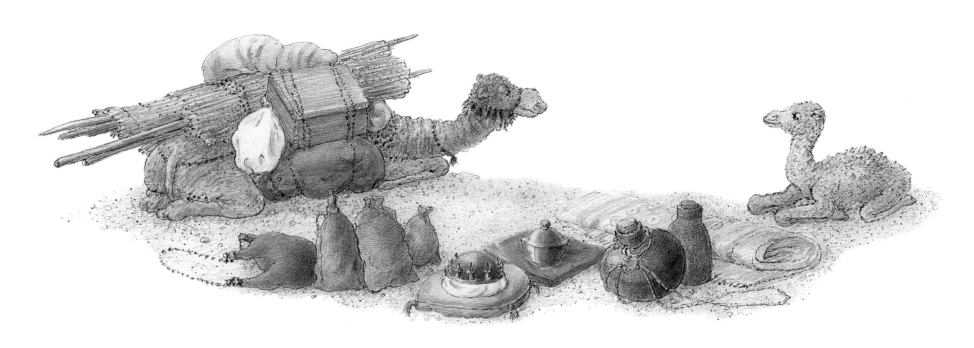

Floris
Books

There was once a powerful king, who was extraordinarily rich. His crown and jewels were so dazzling that when he travelled with his servants, people would stop to bow down before him.

His name was Melchior, but he was known as the King of Gold.

One night, a wondrous bright star appeared
in the sky.

King Melchior summoned his chief advisor,
Omar, saying, "I will journey where this star leads,
to find the greatest king of all."

Omar was a proud man, who wore a tall hat.
"Really?" he replied. "But no king is greater
than you, your majesty. You are the King of Gold."

"Gather my servants and camels, Omar,"
ordered Melchior. "Tonight we set off across
the desert. My son is old enough to rule in
my place while I am gone."

The king's servants grumbled to each other on
the long journey.

"Where are we going?"

"What can he possibly be looking for?"

When their caravan of camels arrived at a small town
called Bethlehem, they were even more astonished.
The king found a humble family with a new baby.
He took off his crown, and knelt before the little child.

"This is the greatest king of all!" he cried.

But King Melchior's servants just stared. And they
grumbled again when he ordered them to unload his
gift of gold. "Perhaps the desert sun has made him ill,"
they whispered.

A few days later, the caravan of camels and servants started the journey eastwards, towards home. Everyone felt relieved to be returning, especially chief advisor Omar in his tall hat.

A short distance outside Bethlehem they passed a beggar. In the past, Melchior would not have noticed such a man, but this time he stepped down from his magnificent white camel, bowed, and pressed a gold coin into the beggar's outstretched hand.

"Your majesty!" cautioned Omar. "If you give so much away, you will be left with nothing!"

"When I have no more gold," replied Melchior, "I shall give the jewels stitched into my robes." He handed coins to every poor person they met.

My warnings are lost on the wind, thought Omar. *A king with no gold is like any common man, and his advisor is less important than that! Something must be done.*

He started a rumour among the servants that the gold was nearly gone, and the king would not be able to pay them. "We will all go hungry," he whispered.

The rumour spread.

Two nights later, the king ate his evening meal in his splendid tent thinking happily about all the people he had helped.

Omar presented him with a goblet of wine. "For your health, your majesty," he said.

Melchior thought the wine tasted a little bitter, but he soon fell deep asleep.

Hours later, the king woke, shivering. *Where is my fur rug?* he wondered. *Oh, the moon and stars are bright in the sky… The sky? Where is my tent?*

Melchior sat up, suddenly alert. He was alone in the desert, with only a simple brown cloak for warmth. He realised what had happened.

"So, you dare to poison your own king, Omar?" he muttered angrily. He pulled the cloak tight around himself against the cold night and started walking.

At midday, tired and hungry, he arrived at a small village. Men approached, carrying heavy sticks.

"Are you expecting an attack?" asked Melchior.

"A powerful king who rode through our village warned us that a robber might follow his caravan," they replied warily.

Then Melchior knew that his chief advisor had taken his place and set the local people against him. *Omar has betrayed me completely*, he thought. Weak from shock and hunger, he collapsed to the ground.

He dreamed he was kneeling before the baby in Bethlehem again.

"Do not fear anything, King Melchior," said the child. "What you have given away for my sake is worth more than any gold."

Melchior became aware of a coolness on his brow, and opened his eyes. A young woman leant over him, holding a cold compress.

"What is your name?" she asked. It was the first time he had ever been asked this.

"I am Melchior," he replied.

"How strange," said the young woman, doubtfully. "That was also the name of the powerful king who passed this way today."

Melchior wanted to shout that he was the true king, but he was afraid the men with sticks would decide he was a liar and a robber. And then he thought of the child in Bethlehem, and how no one knew that *he* was the true king. A feeling of peace came over him.

"Who I am, and where I am going, only God knows," he said to the young woman. "But let me tell you where I have come from." He recounted the story of the king who followed a star, and found a child king.

The young woman was quiet. Then she said, "I didn't expect to believe you. But I can see the light of that star still shines in your eyes. As you spoke about the child, it was as though I was kneeling before him myself. What is his name?"

"His name is Jesus," answered Melchior.

When he was well, Melchior told the story of the king and the star again and again. The men of the village listened. They laid down their sticks and welcomed him as a brother. They asked for the story over and over, and heard it with wonder.

Then Melchior visited more small villages and towns. Some people were suspicious at first, but he found shelter with gentle folk, who listened to his story with open hearts. Often they said, "You are a magician, sir. We felt as though we shared every step of the king, until we ourselves were kneeling before the child. We cannot thank you enough for this gift."

Time passed. Melchior often thought
of his home. *Has Omar killed my dear son?*
Does Omar rule my kingdom now? I must
return. But will I be recognised? Perhaps
not, as my cloak is full of holes,
my feet are bare, and my beard has grown
long and white.

Eventually he reached his kingdom.
As he entered the city, he asked, "Who is
the ruler here?"

"Don't you know?" came the reply.
"The young prince, son of King Melchior,
has just been crowned king."

Melchior felt a flood of relief. His son
was safe. Omar had not taken his throne.

He went to one of the city's bustling markets. A group
of men were drinking coffee, exchanging news.
"Where are you from, stranger?" they asked.
"Buy me some coffee and I'll tell you," replied Melchior.
Almost immediately, a cup appeared. The men listened
closely while Melchior recounted the story of the child king.

"I promise that if you had seen this child,"
finished Melchior, "like the king in my story,
you would have laid everything you possessed
at his feet – your riches, your wisdom and your
honour. You would have given him everything,
yet from then on, you would feel as rich as
the King of Gold simply by serving him."

The men nodded and their eyes shone,
as though they could see the scene themselves.
And then they waited quietly, as if they expected
the story to continue.

Eventually one of them spoke up. "Don't you know the ending to your own story, stranger?"

"What do you mean?" asked Melchior.

"You are telling the story of our own king, the King of Gold. He set off to follow a star and find the greatest king of all. But he never returned from his journey. After much time had passed, his son, the prince, sent out a party of scouts. They returned to say that a terrible sandstorm had whipped through the desert. The king and his entire caravan of servants, camels and tents were lost, buried in sand. What the desert takes, it does not give back.

"There were forty days of mourning for our king. Then the prince was crowned the new king."

Melchior sat in silence, unable to speak. *So Omar has paid a great price for his treachery*, he thought.

Then another idea occurred to him. *If Omar is gone, I could say who I really am. I could become king again!*

But at that moment, Melchior realised he no longer wanted to be king. He had given up his kingdom even before it was taken from him. The story he had to tell was more valuable than any throne and all the gold in the world.

Indeed, he had to tell it often. News spread
fast that a storyteller had come to the city with
a tale of the old king. People flocked to hear.
The young king learned of the storyteller,
and summoned the old man to his palace.

Melchior was nervous. *My son may recognise me,* he thought. *Will I be welcome?*

The new young king sat behind a curtain, as was the custom. Only his servants gathered around. Melchior relaxed, and told the story he had shared so many times.

"As the king travelled home," he finished, "there was no star to safely guide him and his caravan of servants. They were overtaken by a sandstorm, and lost to us forever."

At that, a clear voice came from behind the curtain: "Why do you lie, storyteller?"

Melchior trembled. How did his son know the truth?

"Leave us," commanded the new young king, and his servants departed the room.

Melchior bowed. "Your Highness, what part of my story do you think is untrue?"

To his great surprise, his son laughed. "I don't believe that King Melchior was lost in the desert. The star did guide him safely home, but he prefers to go unrecognised in his own city."

Melchior stared hard at the ground. "And do you fear that Melchior will reclaim your throne, your Highness?"

"I have nothing to fear," replied the king. "My throne is yours to take if you want it, my honoured father. I will serve you, as you serve the child in Bethlehem."

Melchior looked up and saw his son's eyes were shining with joy. The young king bent down and kissed the old storyteller's brow. Melchior kissed his dear son in return.

There were rumours in the kingdom that the gifted old storyteller was really the missing king. But the young king ruled peacefully and wisely for years, and eventually the rumours were forgotten.

Long afterwards, the King of Gold wandered the markets and bazaars of his land barefoot. He gave people his gift, a gift worth more than gold: the story of the greatest king of all.

Based on a translation by Jonathan Drake

First published in German as *Melchior und das Gold der Armen*
by Verlag Urachhaus 2017. First published in English in 2019 by Floris Books
Story © 2015 Georg Dreissig. Illustrations © 2017 Maren Briswalter
English version © 2019 Floris Books
British Library CIP data available ISBN 978-178250-601-0
Printed in China through Asia Pacific Offset Ltd.